Parachuting Hamsters
and
Andy
Russell

Parachuting Hamsters
and
Andy Russell

David A. Adler

With illustrations by
Will Hillenbrand

SCHOLASTIC INC.

New York Toronto London Auckland Sydney
Mexico City New Delhi Hong Kong Buenos Aires

ISBN 0-439-32516-1

12 11 10 9 8 7 6 5 4 3 2   2 3 4 5 6 7/0

Printed in the U.S.A.   40

First Scholastic printing, March 2002

Text set in Century Old Style
Designed by Kaelin Chappell

To Barbara and Elliot,
Etan and Adina

Contents

Parachuting Hamsters
and
Andy Russell

Chapter 1
Eddie Quit?

S he has no pets?" Andy Russell said. He turned and looked directly at his friend Tamika Anderson. "No games, no toys, and no TV? What will we do all weekend?"

It was Friday afternoon. Andy and Tamika were in the backseat of Andy's father's car. They were on their way to Tamika's aunt Mandy and uncle Terence's apartment. Andy and Tamika were going to spend the weekend with them.

"My aunt Mandy says she lives in the most

1

exciting city in the world," said Tamika. "She goes to museums and restaurants, and when I visit, that's where she takes me."

"There's a great natural history museum in the city, with lots of dinosaur skeletons. Maybe we can go there," Andy said. "There's a zoo, and you know what a zoo is? It's a live-animal museum. And I *love* pizza restaurants. Going to museums and restaurants could be fun."

"Sure it will," Tamika said, "even if the museum just has pictures and statues in it and the restaurant doesn't serve pizza."

"No animals? No pizza?"

"You'll see," Tamika reassured Andy, "you'll have a good time. But you should know, my aunt Mandy believes in proper etiquette."

"Aha!" Andy declared, as if he had just made some great discovery. "And I know why proper Eddie quit—he quit because he wanted to go to a zoo and eat pizza."

"Et-i-quette!" Tamika said very slowly. "It means good manners. And Aunt Mandy has lots of rules about how to sit in a restaurant, how to ask for things, and how a guest should behave in her home."

2

Andy looked at his father. "Maybe this isn't such a good idea," Andy said to him. "I'm not always good with all that please-and-thank-you stuff. And I don't know if I'll survive a whole weekend without animals, pizza, games, and television. Maybe Tamika should go to Aunt Mandyland without me."

"Give it a try," Mr. Russell encouraged Andy. "A weekend isn't such a long time. Tamika's aunt and uncle are expecting you."

" 'Give it a try!' " Andy repeated. "That's what you told me when I didn't want to go the first day of kindergarten. 'Give school a try!' Well, I gave it a try. That was more than four years ago and I'm *still* trying. You know, a kid can get tired of giving things a try—especially *this* kid."

Mr. Russell promised, "You won't be at Aunt Mandy's that long."

They were driving across a bridge now, on their way into the city. Andy looked out the car window. "Would it would be bad *Eddie-quit* if I changed my mind?" he asked.

"Yes, it would," Mr. Russell told him.

"Hmmmm," Andy said. He looked across the river, at the tall buildings in the city, and said softly, "How do you do? It's so very nice to meet you and so kind of you to invite me into your beautiful home. May I please kiss your hand?"

Honk! Honk!

There was a lot of traffic on the bridge. Drivers were impatient. The woman in the car behind Mr. Russell was banging on her horn.

Mr. Russell shook his head. There was nothing he could do. There was a long line of slowly moving cars ahead.

Andy kissed the door lock.

"Your hand is really cold," Andy said, "but thank you so very much for letting me kiss it. Thanks a million, a billion, a trillion gazillion! And you're very welcome, too."

"Why are you talking to a car window?" Tamika asked Andy.

"I'm practicing," Andy answered. "And did you notice how polite I was to the window? I said please. I said thank you, and I even kissed the car window's hand."

"You're cashews!" Tamika told him. "Totally nuts!"

"I may be salty and curved, with points at each

end like a cashew, but I'm a *polite* nut. I'm very polite."

"You sure are salted," Tamika said, and pointed to her head. "Real salted."

Honk!

Andy looked back. A large bus was behind them now and the driver had honked.

Andy looked around. Their car was surrounded by other cars, taxicabs, and delivery trucks. He looked at the sidewalks and saw lots of people walking and others waiting at corners to cross the street. He looked at the many tall buildings.

"It's happening again," Andy said. "Every time I come to the city, I feel like a teeny-tiny feeder fish!"

Andy had a pet snake named Slither. It ate feeder fish, minnows he bought at a pet shop.

"Andy, why do you think you're a feeder fish?" Mr. Russell asked patiently.

"Look around you, Dad! This place is stuffed with people! People walking. People riding in cars. People in buildings."

"But no fish," Mr. Russell said.

"In a pet shop there are regular pet fish and feeder fish," Andy explained. "When you buy a regular fish, you point and say, 'I want that one.'

6

When you buy feeder fish, you just say, 'I want ten.' No one cares which ten. To pet-shop people, one feeder fish is the same as another. And with so many people here, I feel like just another feeder fish."

"Well, you're not," Mr. Russell told Andy. "Each person in this city is an individual, and so are you. And even if you and Tamika were both feeder fish, if I came to a pet shop I'd say, 'I know exactly which fish I want. I want the cute boy fish with the reddish-brown hair and the pretty girl fish with the curly black hair.' "

"Thank you," Tamika said.

"Yeah, thanks, Dad," Andy said. "Just don't leave me too long in that fish tank. I don't want my skin to get all wrinkly. And please, don't leave me too long at Aunt Mandy's. Who knows? Maybe my skin will get wrinkly from all that please-and-thank-you stuff."

Mr. Russell turned the corner. This street was not as busy as the last one. There were a few trees along the sidewalk.

"There it is!" Tamika called out. "There's Aunt Mandy's building!"

Chapter 2
Make This Stop!

It was a tall building, set back from the street, with a circular drive in front. Mr. Russell turned onto the drive and stopped by the front door. A man in a blue-and-red uniform held the door open. Andy, Tamika, and Mr. Russell walked in. Andy and Tamika each carried a small suitcase.

People in the lobby were hurrying to the elevator. Others were sitting in large comfortable chairs. A small dog walked by, followed by a man holding its leash.

"Can I help you?" a woman asked. She was wearing a blue-and-red uniform, too, and sitting on a tall stool behind a large, high desk facing the entrance. Behind her were lots of small wooden cubbyholes. Some had folded papers in them.

"We're here to see the Taylors," Mr. Russell told her.

The woman smiled at Andy and Tamika and said, "You must be the children who will be staying with them. Mrs. Taylor will be here soon." The woman took a large envelope from one of the cubbies, gave it to Tamika, and said, "She left this for you. It's something to do while you wait."

Andy and Tamika sat on a couch in the lobby. Mr. Russell sat across from them. Tamika opened the envelope and took out two coloring books and a box of crayons.

"That's what she left us?" Andy said. "Your aunt Mandy must think we're three years old!"

Tamika laughed. "Aunt Mandy doesn't know much about children. When I was four, I spent the night here and do you know what she bought for me? Diapers!"

"Diapers!" Andy exclaimed in shock. "I hope you were polite and thanked her when she put them on you. I hope you said, 'Thank you for wiping my—' "

"NO!" Tamika said before Andy could finish. "Of course not! I told her I didn't need them, but I don't think she believed me. She put a towel on her living room couch and made me sit on it, and every time I got up, she looked to see if it was wet."

Andy looked at his coloring book. It was unlike any he had ever seen before. Each page had outlines of parts of famous paintings with information about the artist.

On one page there was an outline of a smiling woman. Andy colored her face green and her hair purple. He gave her yellow and red eyes, a blue neck, and an orange dress.

"You're beautiful," Andy told the picture. Then he said, "Thank you." He tried to keep his lips from moving when he said it.

"You're getting better at that ventriloquist stuff," Tamika told him. "It almost seemed the picture was talking."

Andy pressed his lips together. "Hello, Tamika," he said, and tried not to move his lips. "It's your aunt Mandy. I'm so glad you could come."

Mr. Russell turned to see who was talking. He was facing the window now. "Oh my," Mr. Russell said when he looked through the window. "I left my car in the drive in front of the building. I should check with the doorman if that's OK."

Andy and Tamika watched through the window while Mr. Russell spoke to the doorman. Then they saw Mr. Russell look beyond the doorman. Andy and Tamika looked, too. Something tied to a small square of yellow cloth, like a parachute, floated to the ground.

Andy and Tamika ran outside to Mr. Russell.

"What was that?" Andy asked.

"I don't know," Mr. Russell answered, "but here comes another one."

Something tied to a small square of red cloth was slowly floating down. This something was right above them.

"It's furry," Andy said as it got closer.

"And I see feet," Tamika added.

It was just a few stories above them now.

"It's wriggling!" Andy said. "It's a live animal." He held his hand open and caught the floating animal before it hit the ground.

"It's a hamster," Andy announced. "It looks scared, *real* scared, but it isn't hurt."

The ends of four thin strings were each tied to one of the hamster's feet. The other ends were each tied to a corner of the square of shiny red cloth.

Andy hurried across the circular drive and carefully picked up the other hamster, the one with the yellow parachute, and announced, "This one's OK, too."

Tamika said, "Here comes another one."

Andy and Mr. Russell looked up and saw it way above them. It was tied to a blue cloth and was slowly getting closer. Something green followed it.

"I'll catch the blue one," Tamika said.

"And I'll get the green one," Mr. Russell said.

The doorman went to Andy and gently petted one of the hamsters.

"Look at this," Andy said, and showed the doorman the red parachute and how the animal's feet were tied to it. "These are living things with hearts and feelings, and look what someone did to them."

Tamika reached up and caught the hamster dangling from the blue parachute. Mr. Russell hurried across the drive, reached up, and caught the one attached to the green parachute.

"Here comes another one," Tamika announced.

"Make this stop!" Andy pleaded with the door-man. "Make this stop!"

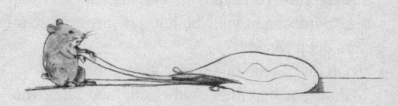

Chapter 3
Oh My Goodness!

I'm sorry. There's nothing I can do," the door
man told Andy. "Speak to Stephanie. She's the
woman inside at the desk. Maybe she can help."

Mr. Russell caught the next hamster. It was tied
to a square of purple cloth.

Andy, Tamika, and Mr. Russell looked up and
waited. When they saw no more hamsters floating
down, Mr. Russell said, "I think that's it."

The doorman held the door open for them as
they walked into the building again. Andy was the

first one inside. He stopped for a moment and told the doorman, "Please, call us if you see any more parachuting hamsters."

Andy showed Stephanie the animals and told her, "Someone in your building is throwing hamsters out a window."

"Oh my," Stephanie said. "That's horrible."

"It sure *is* horrible," Andy said, "and I bet whoever threw these down has lots more hamsters. You know, if you have a few, before you know it you have lots more."

Stephanie took one of the hamsters, held it gently, and examined the strings and the yellow parachute.

"Hamsters are like gerbils," Andy told her. "And I have gerbils. I started with two and now I have about fifty."

"First we have to cut these strings off," she said. "Then we have to find a box or cage for the hamsters and someplace to keep them."

Stephanie took a small pair of scissors from under the counter. She carefully cut the strings tied to the hamster she was holding. Then she gave the scissors to Andy. While Andy cut the red cloth off his hamster, Stephanie picked up the telephone handset and spoke into it, "Tom, I need a box—a deep one."

Andy handed Tamika the scissors.

Stephanie looked at the yellow cloth and the red one Andy gave her. She said, "These are fancy silk handkerchiefs, the kind men wear in the front pockets of their jackets."

A door behind the front counter opened, and a very tall, heavy man in blue coveralls entered the lobby. He was carrying a large wooden box and asked Stephanie, "Is this what you need?"

It was a deep box, with a picture of a wine bottle and WHITE ZINFANDEL printed on one side.

"Yes, that's perfect," Stephanie said.

The man set the box on the floor. Then he introduced himself to Mr. Russell and the children. "My name is Tom," he said. "I'm the building superintendent."

Tom looked at the hamsters and asked Mr. Russell, "Are these animals yours?"

"No," Andy quickly answered for his father. Then he said, "Well, maybe they are. We caught them. We saved them."

While Tom carefully placed the hamsters in the box, Mr. Russell explained what had happened.

Andy, Tamika, Mr. Russell, and Tom looked in the box and watched the hamsters run from one side to the other. They saw one hamster climb on top of another, trying to get out.

Tom said, "These hamsters need a water bottle and some food."

"And wood shavings for the bottom of the box," Andy said, "and toys and tunnels to play with."

"Is there a pet shop nearby?" Mr. Russell asked.

"There's one two blocks from here," Stephanie said.

"Tamika! Tamika!" someone called.

Everyone turned and saw a tall woman standing by the entrance to the lobby. There was a briefcase on the floor at her side. Her arms were stretched out.

"Aunt Mandy," Tamika said, and ran into the woman's arms.

She held Tamika and kissed her on each cheek. Then she picked up her briefcase, took Tamika's hand, and went to the front counter to meet Andy and Mr. Russell.

Tamika's aunt reached out, took Mr. Russell's hand, shook it firmly, and told him, "I'm Mandy Taylor."

"And I'm Charles Russell. This is my son, Andy."

Aunt Mandy wrapped both arms around Andy. She hugged him, and Andy felt his feet lift off the floor.

"Yikes," Andy said. "You're strong."

"What did you say?" Aunt Mandy asked as she put Andy down.

Etiquette, Andy told himself. *I must be polite.*

"I'm very pleased to meet you," Andy said to Aunt Mandy. "Thank you so much for letting me visit you."

"I am sure that having you here will be my pleasure," Aunt Mandy responded. She also greeted Stephanie and Tom.

Go on, Andy thought, *hug Tom. I want to see you lift* him *off his feet!*

But Aunt Mandy didn't hug Tom. She just smiled at him and looked in the box.

"Hamsters?" Aunt Mandy asked.

"We found them outside the building," Andy told her. "They were tied to handkerchiefs and floating down."

"Hamsters with parachutes?" Aunt Mandy asked.

"It seems," Stephanie explained, "someone in our building thought it would be fun to tie them by their feet to handkerchiefs and throw them out a window."

"Children and pets!" Aunt Mandy exclaimed. "Children are just too young to be responsible for other living creatures."

I'm a child and I'm responsible, Andy thought.

"They keep their pets in cages," Aunt Mandy said, "and think they're being nice to them. Animals belong in forests and jungles."

That's a good point, Andy thought. *Am I being nice to Slither, my pet gerbils, and Sylvia the fish? Maybe I should let them go.*

"I'm sure these hamsters were born in a pet shop somewhere," Tom said. "They couldn't survive in a forest."

That's right, Andy decided. *I'm protecting my pets. I feed them, too, and give them lots of toys. They're happy.*

"Tom, will you take care of the hamsters?" Aunt Mandy asked.

"Yes."

"Good," Aunt Mandy said.

"Be good," Mr. Russell whispered to Andy.

Then he told Aunt Mandy, "It's really very nice of you to invite Andy to spend the weekend here. Thank you." He brought Andy and Tamika their suitcases and the coloring books.

"Hey, Dad," Andy said, "aren't you going to the pet shop to buy food and things for the hamsters?"

Mr. Russell looked at Tom. Then he looked at the hamsters. "OK," he said. "I'll go to the pet shop to get food and a water bottle for them." Then Mr. Russell said good-bye, and left.

Aunt Mandy led Andy and Tamika to the elevator. "I have planned a weekend for you filled with wonderful things to do," she said. "When Uncle Terence gets home, we're going to an elegant French restaurant for dinner. Tomorrow morning we're viewing the sculpture exhibit at the Eitan Joshua Museum, and in the afternoon we're going to the ballet."

"French food!" Andy said real loud. "Sculpture! Ballet! That's not kid stuff. That's for old people."

Aunt Mandy smiled and told Andy, "You'll see. You'll like it. Tamika does."

Andy told himself, *This is a BIG mistake. I don't belong in Mandyland!*

Andy looked at Aunt Mandy. She was still smiling. He panicked. "Oh my goodness!" he shouted. "I forgot something!"

Andy grabbed his suitcase and hurried toward the door.

Chapter 4
Detective Andy Russell

The doorman opened the front door. Andy looked for his father's car. It was gone.

He sure got away fast, Andy thought as he walked slowly back toward Aunt Mandy and Tamika. *Great! I'm stuck here with French food, sculpture, ballet, and all this please-and-thank-you stuff.*

"What did you forget?" Aunt Mandy asked as she led Tamika and Andy to the elevator.

"What did I forget?" Andy repeated, thinking of some way to answer that question. "I forgot that I wanted to go with my dad to the pet shop, to get things for the hamsters."

"I'm sure he'll know what to buy," Aunt Mandy said as the elevator door opened. "And while he's at the pet shop, I'll give you a nice snack and get you settled."

They rode up to the eighteenth floor. Then Andy and Tamika followed Aunt Mandy to her apartment.

Inside, two large paintings hung in the entrance area. Each was a large blotch of blue surrounded by other colors. Andy wondered if the paintings were upside down. He leaned over and looked up at them, but they still didn't look right. *Maybe they're inside out,* Andy thought.

"You'll sleep where you always do, in my study," Aunt Mandy said to Tamika. She told Andy he would stay in the library.

"Just put your things in your rooms while I prepare a snack," Aunt Mandy said.

Tamika took Andy to the library. There was a sofa, a large desk, and bookcases filled with books. Andy put his suitcase beside the sofa and looked at some of the books. Lots of them were mysteries.

Hey! Andy thought. *Those hamsters are a mystery. Who threw them out the window?*

There were a pad and a pen on the desk.

Detective Andy Russell will solve this mystery, Andy said to himself. He wrote *Clues* on the top sheet of the pad. Then he thought for a moment. Andy remembered how scared the hamsters had been. He remembered them floating down along the side of the building, and he wrote his first clues:

Lives high up in the building
Has fancy colored handkerchiefs
Is good at tying tiny knots

Andy couldn't think of any more clues, so he waited outside the library for Tamika to come back. They went together to the front of the apartment. Aunt Mandy was just coming out of the kitchen carrying a tray with glasses of milk, icing-covered cubes with candy sprinkles, small plates, forks, and napkins.

Andy looked suspiciously at the cubes. He didn't know what people who went to French

restaurants ate with milk. "What's inside these, under the sprinkles and icing?" he asked.

"Cake and jelly."

"Are you sure?" Andy asked.

"Well, let's check," Aunt Mandy said. She put the tray on a small table in the hall. She used a fork to cut open one of the cubes. She was right. There *was* cake and jelly inside.

"OK," Andy replied. "It's just that I like to know what I'm eating before I eat it."

"That's very wise of you," Aunt Mandy said.

Yes, Andy told himself, *Detective Andy Russell is very wise*.

Aunt Mandy picked up the tray again and walked through the living room to a sliding glass door. She opened it and stepped out, onto the balcony.

Andy stood by the sliding door and looked out. "Wow!" he said. "I can see the bridge and the river and the whole city."

I bet that with a good set of binoculars, Andy thought, *I could solve lots of mysteries from here*.

The balcony was enclosed by a white metal railing. There was a small round table surrounded by four chairs.

Andy stepped onto the balcony and looked down. "Yikes!" he exclaimed.

The people below looked like tiny moving dolls. The cars and trucks looked like toys. Andy sat on the chair farthest from the edge of the balcony and turned it to face the sliding door. He was determined not to look down again.

Then Andy remembered the hamsters. *They were real high when they were thrown out. Of course, they were scared.* Andy wondered who would do such a mean thing to tiny animals. He hoped Tom would take good care of them. And he hoped whoever threw them down didn't have any more hamsters.

Andy took one of the tiny cakes and bit into it. "Wow! This is great," he said.

"I'm glad you like it," Aunt Mandy said.

Andy ate lots of tiny cakes and drank two glasses of milk to wash them down.

"How are your parents?" Aunt Mandy asked Tamika.

Tamika's parents had been badly hurt in a car accident. While they recovered slowly in a rehabilitation center, Tamika was staying with the Russells.

"They're getting better," Tamika told her aunt.

"I call and talk to them almost every week," Aunt Mandy said. "Your mother sounds fine, but I have such difficulty understanding your father."

"I know," Tamika said softly. "He still has trouble talking."

"But he's getting better," Aunt Mandy said. "I know he is."

When they were done eating, Aunt Mandy looked at her watch. "It will be a while before your uncle gets home," she said. "Would you like to read or listen to music?"

"Oh, please," Andy said. "Don't ask Tamika. She'll want to read, and then what will I do?"

"You can read, too," Aunt Mandy said.

"No, I want to wait downstairs for my father. And I want to see the hamsters."

Aunt Mandy looked at Tamika and asked, "Do you want to do that, too?"

Tamika nodded.

"Well, then, go ahead," she told Andy and Tamika. "You have about an hour. Our reservation at the restaurant is for six o'clock."

"Thanks," Andy said.

Tamika walked through the open sliding door

and back into the apartment. Before Andy followed her, he told Aunt Mandy, "And thanks for the little cakes and milk. The little cakes were real good and the milk was real cold—just the way I like it."

"You are certainly very welcome," she replied. "It is a pleasure to have a real gentleman in my home."

Andy smiled.

How about that? he thought. *Detective Andy Russell is a gentleman, a* real *gentleman.*

Chapter 5
Cashews Are Nuts

A ndy and Tamika rode the elevator down to the lobby. Then Stephanie took them down the back stairs to Tom's office, so they could visit the hamsters.

Tom's office was in the underground garage, just opposite the stairwell. His worktable was cluttered with papers, boxes, a toaster, and other small appliances. There was a broken baby carriage by his table, a tricycle, and a few wooden boxes. Tom had his toolbox open. He was fixing a lamp.

The WHITE ZINFANDEL box was on the floor by Tom's desk. Andy looked in. The hamsters were running in small circles and climbing over one another.

Andy held out the palm of his hand and pretended it was a pad. He pretended his pointing finger on the other hand was a pen. Andy introduced himself to the hamsters. "I'm Detective Russell," he said. "So, who tied the handkerchiefs to your feet? Who threw you out the window?"

Tom stopped working on the lamp and looked at Andy. Tamika looked, too.

The hamsters didn't respond.

"So, you won't talk," Andy said. "How can I help you if you don't answer my questions?" He waited.

The hamsters still didn't respond.

"Well," Andy said, "there are ways to *make* you talk."

"There are?" Tom asked. "I'd like to hear these hamsters talk."

Andy pursed his lips. "We're crowded in here," he said with his lips still together.

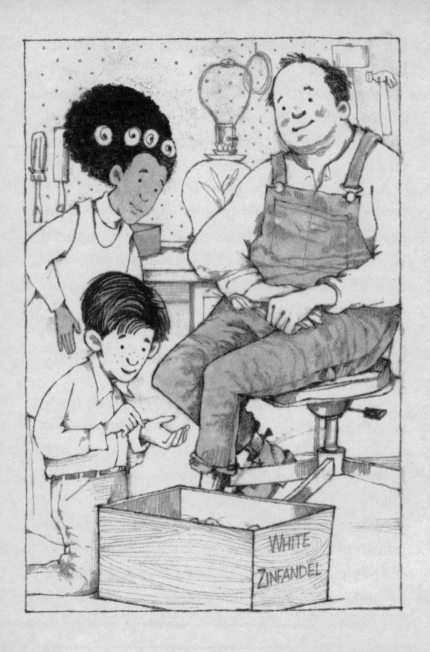

Tom looked at Andy.

"We're crowded," Andy said again, without moving his lips.

Tamika pointed at Andy and said, "Cashews."

"Cashews?" Tom asked. "Cashews are nuts."

"Well?" Tamika asked. "What do you think Andy is?

"I was just practicing being a ventriloquist," Andy explained. "And I was saying they're crowded in there. We need another box so we can split them up."

"No!" Tamika said. "If we split them up, we might be taking hamster children from their parents. I'm sure they'd rather be with their parents in a crowded box than be separated from them."

Andy thought about Tamika being away from *her* parents while they were in the rehabilitation center. He understood why she didn't want Tom to break up the hamster families.

Tom said, "After I fix this lamp, I'll look for a bigger box."

Andy and Tamika watched Tom fix the lamp. He split apart one end of the cord, peeled away plastic coating from the end of the wire, and attached a plug. He pulled the other end of the wire through the lamp and attached the bulb socket and switch. He screwed in a bulb. Then he plugged in the lamp and turned the switch. The light went on. He turned the lamp on and off a few times.

"Fixed," Tom declared. "Fourteen-B will be pleased."

"Fourteen-B?" Andy asked. "What kind of a name is that?"

"It's not a name," Tom explained. "It's an apartment number. I know everyone in this building by his or her apartment. To me Tamika's aunt and uncle are Mr. and Mrs. Eighteen-A."

The door to the stairwell opened. Mr. Russell stepped out. He was carrying a large bag. "I have a bowl, hamster food, and a water bottle," he said.

"Hey, Dad," Andy said, "that's great." He filled the bowl with food and put it in the wooden box. Then, while Tamika was setting up the water bottle, Andy told his father, "I plan to find out who threw out the hamsters. And when I do, I'll ask what he—or maybe she—thinks it would feel like to be tied to a handkerchief and thrown out a window."

Mr. Russell told Andy, "Just don't get into any trouble."

"Me?" Andy said, pretending to be shocked. "Do I ever get into trouble?"

"Yes, all the time," Mr. Russell said. "Just don't get into trouble here."

"OK, Dad."

Andy and Tamika watched as a hamster stretched up and drank from the water bottle. Another went to the food bowl and ate.

"I hope you like your meal," Andy said to the hamsters.

"You really love animals," Tom said to Andy. "Do you want to take these home with you?"

Andy looked at his dad.

Mr. Russell shook his head.

Tamika told Tom, "He already has a snake, gerbils, and a goldfish. That's a lot of pets in one house."

"It sure is," Tom said.

Tamika looked at her watch. It was almost six o'clock. "We have to go now," she said. "My aunt might be waiting for us."

"And I have to get home," Mr. Russell said.

Tamika, Andy, and Mr. Russell went back up the stairs to the lobby.

Andy told his father, "I'm giving Aunt Mandyland a try, and so far it's not so bad."

"Good," Mr. Russell said.

Andy and Tamika said good-bye again to Mr. Russell. The two of them got on the elevator. Tamika pressed the 18 button. Just as the doors started to close, someone wedged his briefcase between them. The doors opened, and a tall man in a dark suit stepped into the elevator with his large leather briefcase.

"Hey, look at you—look at pretty you," the man said. He dropped his briefcase, grabbed Tamika, and lifted her into the air.

Tamika's head almost hit the ceiling of the elevator. She looked down, smiling nervously. "Hi, Uncle Terence."

"And who is this fine-looking young man?" Uncle Terence asked as he put Tamika down. "Is he your friend Andy?"

"Yes," Tamika answered.

"That's me," Andy said, and stepped back. He didn't want Tamika's uncle to pick *him* up. Andy stuck out his hand to shake and said, "Hello, Mr. Taylor. I'm happy to meet you."

"It's Uncle Terence," Tamika's uncle said as he grabbed Andy's hand. "And I'm happy to meet you, too." He squeezed Andy's hand and shook it.

"Hey!" Andy said. "You and Aunt Mandy squeeze and hug real hard."

"We do?" Uncle Terence asked.

Andy wiggled his fingers. They all still worked. "It's OK," he told Uncle Terence. "You just got me by surprise." Andy put his hand in his pocket. He didn't want anyone else in the city to get him by surprise.

"Did Mandy tell you where we're eating dinner?" Uncle Terence asked. "It's a wonderful little French restaurant with great *poulet au poivre vert* and even better creamy, sweet pastries."

"*Pool-per*-what?" Andy asked.

"It's chicken with green pepper—and it's great," Uncle Terence explained just as the elevator doors opened. "Here we are—home sweet home."

As soon as they had entered the apartment, Aunt Mandy said, "We're late," and rushed everyone to the elevator again.

"You must be *real* hungry," Andy said to Aunt Mandy once they were in the elevator.

"It's not that," Aunt Mandy explained. "It's just not polite to be late when you have reservations."

"There sure are a lot of *polite* rules," Andy said.

Aunt Mandy smiled and said, "Yes, I guess there are."

Chapter 6
Watch Out!

It was a long cab ride to the restaurant—past lots of pizza, hamburger, and taco places.

"Look at all these great places we're passing," Andy said. "How about having pizza instead of French food?"

"You'll *like* French food," Uncle Terence told Andy.

I don't think so, Andy thought.

When they arrived at the French restaurant, a

tall man wearing a tuxedo greeted them at the entrance.

"Good evening, Madame and Monsieur Taylor," the man said, and bowed slightly. "It's so good to see you again."

"Good evening, Pierre," Aunt Mandy replied.

Pierre led Aunt Mandy, Uncle Terence, Andy, and Tamika through the dark, crowded restaurant to a small round table in the corner. Two candles flickered from the middle of the table. Pierre raised his hand, and a short fat man in a very tight tuxedo appeared carrying menus. The man's straight black hair seemed to be pasted to his head.

He looks like a penguin—a big menu-carrying penguin, Andy thought, but he didn't say it.

The man looked at Aunt Mandy and Uncle Terence, and then up at the ceiling. "Good evening. I am Jacques," he said formally. "I will be your waiter."

Andy looked up at the ceiling, too, to see who Jacques was talking to, but all he saw were some shadows made by the candles' flickering flames.

Jacques gave everyone at the table a menu,

stepped back, clasped his hands together, held them in front of his belly, and looked up again.

As long as he's looking up there, Andy thought, *I'll give him something fun to see.* Andy linked his two thumbs, stretched out his fingers, and waved them in front of the candles. He was making a shadow puppet of a bird. He looked up again. The flickering candlelight made it seem like the bird was flying. Andy looked at Jacques. The waiter's bored expression hadn't changed.

Andy made a shadow puppet of a ferocious wolf, but Jacques pretended not to notice. *Now what could he be looking at up there?* Andy wondered. He leaned back and tried to get a better look at the ceiling, but he still didn't see anything. Andy stood on his chair, to get a closer look.

"What are you doing?" Tamika whispered.

"Andy, please get down," Aunt Mandy told him.

"I was just trying to see what Jacques was looking at," Andy explained as he sat in his seat again.

"Hmmm," Jacques said.

Hmmm, yourself, Andy thought. He took the twisted cloth napkin from his glass and spread it across his lap. He carefully moved his chair under the table and then looked at his menu.

The menu was coated in plastic. Andy looked at all six pages.

"Hey, I thought this was a French restaurant," Andy complained to Jacques. "You don't have any French fries!"

Still gazing at the ceiling, Jacques said slowly, "We have potatoes, of course, but not fried. We have *purée de pommes de terre, pommes de terre au four,* and *galettes de pommes de terre.*"

"You have what?" Andy asked.

"Mashed potatoes, baked potatoes, and potato pancakes," Uncle Terence explained.

"OK," Andy said. "Please give me potato pancakes."

"That's breakfast food," Tamika said.

Aunt Mandy said, "Tamika is right. Why don't you choose something else?"

Andy told them, "But I like pancakes."

Jacques waited. When Andy didn't change his order, Jacques said, *"Galettes,"* and wrote that on his pad.

"And could I please have applesauce or syrup to put on top of those *gal*-things?" Andy asked.

Jacques looked down at Andy disapprovingly. Then he wrote something on his pad.

"I hope you put down applesauce or syrup," Andy said.

"We have caramel applesauce," Jacques mumbled, still looking down at his pad.

Aunt Mandy, Uncle Terence, and Tamika each ordered *poulet au poivre vert*.

"Very good," Jacques said, and wrote their orders on his pad. Then, with his head up and his eyes still directed at the ceiling, he walked toward the two doors that led to the kitchen.

"In this dark place he should look where he's going," Andy said. "He really should."

When Jacques returned, a helper stood by him with a basket of twisted rolls and a dish of butter.

Andy took a hot roll, cut and buttered it, and then bit into it. "Hey, this is good," he said.

Jacques bowed slightly. With his hands clasped in front of him, he told Andy, "I think you'll find everything here is quite good."

Later, when Jacques brought out the dinners, he carefully placed the plates in front of Uncle Terence, Aunt Mandy, Tamika, and Andy. *"Bon appétit,"* he said as he rotated the plates slightly so they would look just right in front of each diner.

Proper Eddie-quit, Andy told himself as he reached for his fork. *I must use proper Eddie-quit.* He watched Aunt Mandy and did just what she did. He tapped his lips with the edge of his napkin after each forkful of pancake and applesauce. He put his fork down while he swallowed, and he rested after each bite. When he was thirsty, he took only small sips of water.

Now I know why Aunt Mandy was in such a hurry, Andy thought. *She wanted to get started with dinner because it takes so long to eat and drink the polite nibble-and-sip way.* When he had finished his pancakes, Andy told Aunt Mandy and Uncle Terence, "Thanks for the food. It was real good, especially the applesauce."

"Yes," Tamika said. "My dinner was good, too."

Aunt Mandy patted her lips with the edge of her napkin and said, "You are both very welcome."

Uncle Terence smiled and told Andy and Tamika, "Now comes the best part of the meal, the dessert, and I know just what we'll have." He signaled to Jacques and told him, "We'll all have *mousse au chocolat meringuée.*"

"Mouse!" Andy exclaimed. "I don't eat mouse."

"No," Tamika told him, "it's *mousse,* not *mouse.*"

"And I don't eat moose, either. I don't eat animals. Why can't I have a *real* dessert, like cake, ice cream, or pudding?"

"*Mousse au chocolat meringuée is* pudding," Uncle Terence explained. "It's rich chocolate pudding layered with baked egg whites that have been sweetened and whipped. It's delicious."

"Oh," Andy said. "It's just that I like to know what I'm eating before I eat it."

"That's true," Aunt Mandy told Uncle Terence. "He *does* like to know what he's eating."

"Thank you," Jacques said. He looked up, turned, and went to the kitchen.

There he goes again, Andy thought, *looking at the ceiling! He's a real up-looker. Well, one day he'll step in some nasty stuff and learn to look where he's going.*

Just then a woman at the next table coughed. "Oh my," she said, and coughed again, this time really loudly.

Andy turned and looked at her. She was an old woman, with lots of curly white hair. A wooden cane was hooked onto the back of her chair. An old man was sitting with her.

"Drink something," the old man advised the woman.

She took a big gulp of water, but it didn't help. While she was drinking, she coughed again—and water sprayed across the table. The woman's face became very red. The man quickly got up and gently patted her on the back. When he did that, he accidentally knocked the cane to the floor.

"Look," Aunt Mandy said, "here come our desserts."

Jacques was walking toward them, looking up while holding a tray above his head with one hand. Andy couldn't see what was on the tray.

The old woman coughed again, and Andy watched as the old man patted her back again, a little harder this time. She drank some more water. Then Andy looked at Jacques. The waiter was close now, just by the table.

"Watch out, Jacques!" Andy warned. "Watch out!"

The old man and woman turned. The woman coughed and sprayed more water, this time onto Jacques.

Jacques looked at the old woman, at Andy, and at the floor, but he looked too late. He stepped onto the woman's cane. The cane flew up and Jacques fell to the floor. The tray flipped over and crashed down on his pasted-down hair. Chocolate pudding and meringue splattered onto his hair, face, and tuxedo jacket.

The old woman told Jacques, "Oh, I'm so sorry about the water."

"And I'm sorry about the cane," the old man said as he picked it up and again hung it from the back of the chair. "I'm terribly sorry."

"It's not your fault," Jacques declared, pointing a pudding-coated finger at Andy. "It's *his* fault! Children don't belong in restaurants."

"It's not my fault," Andy said. "It's *your* fault. You shouldn't look at the ceiling all the time. You should look where you're going."

Jacques shook his fist at Andy and declared, "And you shouldn't talk back to adults!"

"Andy is right," Aunt Mandy said. "Please, don't yell at him again."

Jacques tried to get up, but he slipped on some pudding.

Pierre hurried from the front of the dining

room to Jacques, reached down, and helped him up. Jacques's helper appeared with a mop and began to clean the floor.

Jacques pointed at Andy and told Pierre, "He shouted and scared me. That's why I fell."

"No, that's not what happened," Aunt Mandy said. "Andy has been a perfect gentleman. You didn't look where you were going. Andy tried to warn you before you tripped on the cane."

Jacques looked at Aunt Mandy and Uncle Terence. Then he picked up the tray and the dishes and carried them into the kitchen.

"I'm terribly sorry," Pierre said. "I hope none of you had your clothes soiled."

Aunt Mandy and Uncle Terence checked. Their clothes were clean. Tamika's clothes were clean, too. Andy's weren't. Some pudding had splattered onto the bottom of his pants leg, but he didn't tell anyone.

"I'll bring you fresh mousse," Pierre said, "and an assortment of cakes and pastries, with my compliments."

When Pierre walked off toward the kitchen doors, Uncle Terence leaned forward and whispered, "Jacques didn't look happy."

"Yeah," Andy said, "but when he was on the floor, he looked funny—like a penguin with a potty accident."

Uncle Terence laughed.

Andy thought for a moment. Then he said, "Oops! I meant a penguin with a *pudding* accident, not a potty accident."

Aunt Mandy patted Andy's hand and told him, "We know what you meant."

Pierre set cups of mousse and meringue in front of Andy, Tamika, Aunt Mandy, and Uncle Terence, and he put a large tray of pastries and cakes covered with icing and filled with jelly and cream in the middle of the table.

Andy looked at the dish of chocolate mousse in front of him and at the tray of cakes and pastries. He didn't know what to eat first. Then he noticed a large round cake covered with chocolate icing and decorated with a pink-icing face that seemed to be smiling up at him.

Andy quickly reached across the table. He got some mousse on his shirtsleeve as he took the smiling cake. Andy bit into the cake and pink cream squirted out. "Oops!" he said, and quickly scooped up the cream with his spoon.

Andy got icing and cream on his hands, chin, and shirt, but he was too busy to wipe it off. Next he ate a square of five-layered multicolored cake, and some jelly from between the layers oozed onto his shirt.

Andy then ate a large heart-shaped cookie covered with powdered sugar. He got sugar all over his hands and pants. Andy looked down at his pants and then up at Aunt Mandy, Uncle Terence, and Tamika. They all were looking at him.

Tamika laughed and told Andy, "You look like someone who had an accident, too—a jelly, sugar, and icing accident."

Andy brushed off his pants. He wiped his lips, chin, and hands with his napkin. Then he took a big spoonful of chocolate mousse and meringue.

Uncle Terence was right, Andy thought. *It* is *delicious.*

Andy and Tamika finished their chocolate mousse and every cake and pastry on the dessert tray. When Andy got up from the table, he felt full—like a balloon about to pop.

On their way out of the restaurant, Aunt Mandy and Uncle Terence thanked Pierre.

"Yeah," Andy added. "Thanks a lot for the great pancakes and desserts. Thanks a *million.*"

They rode by taxi back to the apartment building. It was dark now, but Andy noticed that in the city, at night, there were still lots of lights on—and lots of people outside, on the sidewalks and in cars.

Once they were inside the lobby, Aunt Mandy pressed the button to call the elevator. Andy looked up. A light above the elevator showed that it was at the twentieth floor. They waited. When the elevator came down and the doors opened, Aunt Mandy pressed 18.

"Oh my," she said, and looked at her finger. "This is greasy!" She held it in front of her nose. "It smells like butter," she said. "Someone got butter on the elevator button." Aunt Mandy took a tissue from her purse and wiped her finger.

Uncle Terence looked at the control panel and said, "Someone spread butter on *all* the buttons!"

Parachuting hamsters and buttered elevator buttons? Andy thought. *Probably the same person did both. I've got to add this to my list of clues.*

"What a greasy mess," Aunt Mandy said as she took another tissue from her purse.

"This is an interesting building," Andy sai[d]. "Maybe tomorrow someone will butter the lobby floor and people will slide out of the building."

"This is a good building," Aunt Mandy told him. "There are just strange things going on here."

There sure are, Andy thought. *I wonder what will happen here tomorrow.*

Chapter 7
Beep! Beep!

The next morning Andy looked out the library window. He didn't see any people sliding out of the building. He was disappointed.

At breakfast Aunt Mandy told Andy and Tamika, "First, we'll go to the Eitan Joshua Museum to see the sculpture exhibit. We'll have lunch, and then we'll be off to the ballet. Uncle Terence can't come along. He has to work, but Jason Collins will join us. I thought it would be nice for Andy to meet him—he lives upstairs and is about your age."

When Aunt Mandy went to the kitchen for some more milk, Tamika whispered to Andy, "I've met Jason Collins and I don't like him. He's spoiled and mean."

After breakfast, when they got in the elevator, Aunt Mandy pushed the button for the twentieth floor.

"No butter?" Andy asked.

"No," Aunt Mandy answered. "No butter."

Andy and Tamika stood beside Aunt Mandy as she knocked on the door of apartment 20-B.

"Who is it?" someone asked from the other side of the door.

"It's Mandy Taylor, with my niece Tamika and her friend Andy. We're here to pick up Jason."

A woman wearing a pink uniform and an apron opened the door.

Aunt Mandy said, "Hello, Doris," and introduced Andy and Tamika.

Doris smiled. "I'll get Jason," she said, and left. She soon returned, followed by a boy riding in a motorized toy car.

Jason pressed the knob in the center of the steering wheel.

Beep! Beep!

Jason said, "Hello, Mandy."

Aunt Mandy replied, "Hello, Jason. I'm sure you remember my niece Tamika, and this is her friend Andy."

"So what?" Jason asked. Before anyone could respond, he honked his horn again. *Beep! Beep!* "I'll be right back," he said as he turned his toy car around and drove off. Tamika nudged Andy and gave him an I-told-you-so look.

Jason returned without his car. He was carrying a backpack.

Aunt Mandy looked at the backpack and said to Jason, "You don't need to bring anything along. We're going to a restaurant for lunch."

Jason gripped his backpack tightly. "This isn't food. It's *other* stuff," he said quickly.

Other stuff? Andy thought. *What other stuff?*

Aunt Mandy smiled and said, "OK, let's go."

Andy saw Tom in the lobby. He asked him about the hamsters.

"They're fine," Tom said. "They're so much fun to watch."

Tamika told Jason about the hamsters.

"Parachuting hamsters?" Jason said in wonderment. "Just like marines."

"They were scared," Andy said.

The children followed Aunt Mandy outside. The doorman blew a whistle and a taxi pulled up. Aunt Mandy got in the front seat. The children got in the back. Tamika went in first, then Andy. Jason got in last and put his backpack between him and Andy.

What's in that backpack? Andy wondered. *This is a job for Detective Russell!* He slowly moved his right hand to his side and tried to feel what was inside the backpack. *There's something hard and round in here, like a can.*

Jason saw that Andy was touching his backpack. He glared at him, then pulled the pack away and put it on his lap.

The taxicab stopped in front of a large building with lots of tall stone columns and a huge staircase leading up to several revolving doors.

Aunt Mandy paid the driver. Then she opened the cab door and said, "Here we are."

Tamika, Andy, and Jason followed her up the stairs. There was a tall arch inside the revolving doors, a metal detector with a guard standing beside it.

Aunt Mandy, Andy, and Tamika walked through

the metal detector. They waited for Jason. He looked at the sides and then up at the top of the arch. Then he walked slowly through it.

Beep! Beep!

"What's in the backpack?" the guard asked.

"Just some stuff," Jason answered.

"Please, open it."

Jason lifted the backpack onto the table by the metal detector and slowly unzipped it. The guard looked in. Andy moved closer to Jason. He tried to look in the backpack, too. Jason glared at Andy again and Andy moved away. He walked to the other side of Aunt Mandy.

The guard told Jason, "You'll have to leave this here."

Jason reached into the pack. He took out some paper and a marker and asked, "Can I take this in?"

"OK, kid," the guard said. Then he took the backpack and put it on a shelf behind him with lots of other bags and backpacks. He gave Jason a tag with a number on it. Jason joined Aunt Mandy, Andy, and Tamika, and they entered the main entrance hall of the Eitan Joshua Museum.

The hall was enormous. At the very front was a

large bronze statue of a man leaning on a walking stick. The statue showed the man smiling, with a derby on his head and a large mustache that curled at the ends, beneath his nose.

"That's Eitan Joshua," Aunt Mandy said. "He owned a whole fleet of ocean liners and tugboats. He was a very rich man, and he traveled all over the world. Wherever he went, if he saw something he liked—especially a painting or piece of sculpture—he bought it. He established this museum almost one hundred years ago, so anyone who wanted to could see his great art collection."

"Hello, Mr. Joshua," Andy said, and bowed. "Thank you for inviting us to your museum."

Jason looked at Andy.

"Yesterday he talked to a car window," Tamika said.

"Yes, I did," Andy admitted. "I was polite to the window and now I'm being polite to Mr. Eitan Joshua." He turned to the statue and asked, "Isn't that right?"

"That's right," Andy said. He pursed his lips and tried to speak from his diaphragm, throwing his voice the way ventriloquists do. But it didn't work.

"Your lips moved," Tamika said.

"Aha!" Andy said. "That's because this time Eitan Joshua was the ventriloquist. His lips didn't move, did they? And he made it seem like *I* was talking." He turned and told the statue, "Good job, Eitan Joshua."

"That's sure right," Jason told Andy. "That statue was the ventriloquist and you were his dummy."

Now it was Andy who glared at Jason.

"Let's go in and look at the exhibits," Aunt Mandy said. She and the children walked around Eitan Joshua and past paintings of bowls of fruits and vases of flowers to a very large open hall with a high ceiling. The room was filled with stone and metal statues. There were wooden benches along the sides of the room.

"There are some magnificent pieces here," Aunt Mandy said.

Andy and Tamika walked around a large white marble L-shaped statue. They looked at the plaque for it: BENT FORM, DEB NESHER. Next they looked at a pile of large squares of white marble and its plaque: BROKEN OBELISK, DEB NESHER.

Andy said, "Deb Nesher seems to like bent and broken things." He looked across the room at

Jason, who was walking slowly around a tall, white marble statue of a man leaning against a stone column.

"What do you think is in his backpack?" Andy asked Tamika.

"I don't know," Tamika answered. "Maybe it's some kind of security thing, like a blanket. You know—something he takes with him wherever he goes."

"Maybe," Andy said. "But if it *is* a security thing, he keeps it in a can. I felt his backpack and I think he has a can in there."

Jason walked behind the statue and stayed there awhile.

Tamika said, "He seems to like the back of the statue more than the front of it."

Andy and Tamika watched Jason and waited.

"Look at him now," Tamika said. "He's walking real fast to the other side of the room."

"He did something to that marble man," Andy said. "I'm sure of it."

Andy and Tamika walked across the exhibit hall, to the statue Jason had been looking at. Andy looked up at the marble man, and the marble man seemed to look down at Andy. Tamika walked to the back of the statue.

"What did he do to you, Marble Man?" Andy asked.

"Look in the back. Look what he did."

Andy was startled. "You talk?" he asked the statue.

"No, *I* talk," Tamika said, and grabbed Andy's hand. She pulled him to the other side of the statue.

A sheet of paper was stuck with chewing gum to the back of the statue. Written on the paper was: *Help! Get me out of here! I'm being held prisoner in this stupid museum.*

"Do you think that's funny?" Tamika asked.

"No," Andy answered.

"I'm going to tell one of the guards," Tamika said. She walked toward the entrance to the hall, where a guard was standing.

Andy caught up with Tamika and grabbed her arm. "If you tell the guard, he'll ask you who did it," he said. "You'll tell them Jason did. He'll get in trouble and so will Aunt Mandy. She brought him here, so she's responsible for him. We'll all be kicked out of the museum and your aunt won't like that."

Tamika stopped. "So what should we do?" she asked.

"We have to be like detectives and watch him," Andy said. "We have to keep him—and us and Aunt Mandy—out of trouble."

It was a large exhibit hall, with lots of large statues and people standing around many of them. The statues hid some of the people from Andy and Tamika's view.

"There he is," Andy said, and pointed to the far end of the hall. "Jason's looking at that statue of a horse with its front legs up in the air." He told Tamika, "You're with Detective Andy Russell now. Just do what I do."

Tamika followed Andy to the large metal statue. When they got to the front of it, Jason walked to the back. Andy and Tamika slowly walked toward the back, and Jason walked around the other side of the horse, to the front. Then he stopped and turned to face Andy and Tamika.

"Why are you following me?" he asked.

"We're looking at a statue," Andy told him.

"That's why we came to the museum. And if you don't like it, that's just too bad!"

Jason walked across the exhibit hall.

Andy and Tamika followed him.

"Oh, there you are," Aunt Mandy said to all three children. "I've been looking for you. I want to show you something." She led them to a large stone sculpture. "Look what the artist did here," she continued. "You can almost see the human form, emerging from the rock. The form and the stone are in complete harmony."

"That's nice," Jason said.

Aunt Mandy talked on and on about the statue and the artist.

Jason stood close to Aunt Mandy and pretended to be really interested in what she was saying.

He's such a phony, Andy thought.

Tamika poked Andy. "Look," she whispered. "Look over there."

A guard had discovered Jason's mischief. He was standing behind Marble Man, shaking his head and talking into a walkie-talkie.

Aunt Mandy turned and looked at another statue. "This one is by the same artist," she said.

"Here the form and stone are in harmony, too. What do you think of it?"

"It's lovely," Jason answered.

Andy and Tamika didn't answer. They were watching what was happening with Marble Man.

The guard and a woman carrying a clipboard had gathered around Marble Man. Then a woman wearing coveralls and carrying a large toolbox appeared. Other people who were visiting the museum stood around the sculpture, too.

"Well, Tamika and Andy, what do you think?" Aunt Mandy asked again.

"He should be arrested," Andy replied.

"What!" Aunt Mandy said in shock. "Just because you don't like a piece of art is no reason to say the artist should be arrested."

"Oh, sorry," Andy said. He realized that Aunt Mandy was talking about the statue in front of them and not about Marble Man.

"That's right," Jason said, and smiled.

The woman in coveralls carefully pulled the paper off Marble Man. She opened her toolbox, took out a can, and sprayed the back of the statue. Then she wiped it with a towel.

Aunt Mandy walked around to another statue.

"We know you put that sign on Marble Man," Andy whispered to Jason, "and we think it's disgusting."

"You don't know anything," Jason replied.

The woman with the clipboard spoke to the guard. The guard looked around. He started to move through the exhibit hall, looking closely at the visitors. Then he walked toward Andy, Tamika, Jason, and Aunt Mandy.

"I'm hungry and thirsty," Jason said quickly to Aunt Mandy. "Could I get something to eat and drink?"

"I had planned to take you to a nice restaurant," Aunt Mandy answered, "but if you're hungry now, we can go to the museum cafeteria."

Chapter 8
Andy Russell Was Here!

There were lots of white tables surrounded by white plastic chairs in the museum cafeteria. But other than two women sitting at one of the tables and drinking coffee, the seats were empty. A large counter in front, with a sign above it, listed the menu:

HOT DOGS
HAMBURGERS

FRENCH FRIES
POTATO CHIPS
ICE CREAM
FRUIT
SODA
MILK
JUICE, COFFEE, TEA

"What would you like?" Aunt Mandy asked Tamika, Andy, and Jason when they reached the counter. A man stood there, ready to take their order.

"I want potato chips," Andy answered.

"And I would like an apple," Tamika said.

Then Jason said, "I want ice cream, French fries, and a can of orange soda."

Aunt Mandy placed the order and told the man she wanted a cup of coffee.

The food was put on two trays. Andy and Tamika each carried a tray to the table they all shared. Jason looked at the food he had ordered and said, "I have to go to the bathroom."

"Hurry back," Aunt Mandy told him, "before the ice cream melts."

"I will," Jason said, and quickly left the cafeteria.

"You have to go, too," Tamika whispered to Andy. "You have to follow him."

"No, I don't. I went before we left the apartment."

"*Yes, you do,*" Tamika insisted. "You have to make sure he doesn't get into trouble."

"Oh, that's right," Andy said loud enough for Aunt Mandy to hear. "I have to go to the bathroom, too. May I be excused?"

"Yes, you may," Aunt Mandy told him.

Andy hurried out of the cafeteria. In the hall he found a door marked MEN. He opened it and went in. Andy looked around. The bathroom appeared to be empty. *Maybe he went somewhere else*, he thought. *Maybe he's sticking a note on one of the paintings—or on the Eitan Joshua statue or on a sleeping guard.* Andy was about to leave the bathroom when he heard a squeaking sound.

Eeek!

Andy stopped.

Eeek!

The noise was coming from the second stall. The door was closed, but Andy saw a pair of sneakers—and they weren't set on the floor the

way they would be if someone were using the toilet. He watched the sneakers. They moved to the right.

Eeek!

Eeek!

The sneakers moved again—this time toward the door to the stall.

Andy quickly went to the sink and turned on the water. He looked in the mirror above the sink and watched the door to the second stall. When Andy saw the door open, he put his hands under the running water and started to wash them.

Jason came out of the stall, saw Andy, and asked, "Hey, what are you doing here?"

"You needed to use the bathroom and so did I," Andy answered.

Jason was about to leave the bathroom.

"Aren't you going to wash your hands?" Andy asked.

"Oh," Jason said, and he joined Andy at the sink.

Andy noticed red marks on Jason's hands.

Jason washed his hands with soap and the marks came off.

"Let's go," Jason told Andy. "I'm done and so are you."

As they moved past the stalls, Jason walked between Andy and the doors to the stalls. Andy tried to look into the one Jason had been in, but Jason was in his way.

"You did something in there, didn't you?" Andy asked.

"Of course I did! That's why I came to the bathroom!"

When Andy and Jason returned to the table in the cafeteria, Tamika whispered to Andy, "What did he do?"

"I don't know, but he got red stuff all over his hands."

As Andy ate his potato chips, he watched Jason.

Jason dipped one of his French fries into the cup of vanilla ice cream, then ate it. He drank some orange soda, then dipped more French fries into the ice cream and ate them, too.

Aunt Mandy put down her cup of coffee and said, "We're going to see the Impressionist paintings next." Then she, too, watched Jason eat. "That's an interesting combination—potatoes and ice cream."

"Ang ins genichus," Jason said with his mouth

full. He swallowed. "And it's delicious," he said again.

When they left the cafeteria, Andy said, "I'll be right back." He hurried into the bathroom and opened the door to the second stall. ANDY RUSSELL WAS HERE! was written in red marker across one of the tile walls.

Now he's trying to get me *in trouble,* Andy thought. *I hate him.* He rubbed the red-printed ANDY and it smudged. He rubbed harder—and it smudged more.

At least he didn't use a permanent marker, Andy thought as he hurried to the sink. He pulled two paper towels from the dispenser, wet them, and returned to the second stall. He rubbed Jason's message again and smudged it some more.

Andy threw the two paper towels out and pulled two more from the dispenser. He wet them, and this time he squirted on some liquid soap.

The bathroom door opened. One of the guards entered. He smiled at Andy as he walked into the bathroom. But as he passed the second stall, he stopped. "What's this?" he asked. The guard went into the stall—and quickly came out. He pointed

76

to the writing on the wall and asked Andy, "Did you do that?"

"No, sir."

"What's your name?" the guard asked.

"Andy Russell."

"That's the name on the wall," the guard told Andy. "Now, you wash that off."

"That's what I'm doing," Andy said, showing the guard the wet paper towels.

The guard watched as Andy scrubbed the wall some more.

When Andy went to get more towels, he told the guard, "Someone else wrote this to get me in trouble."

"Well," the guard said in an angry voice, "you *are* in trouble."

"Look," Andy said, "check me. I don't have a red marker. I don't have *any* marker." He pulled his pockets inside out, to show they were empty.

"OK," the guard said in a gentler voice, "just clean the wall."

Andy scrubbed until all the red marker was gone. Then he asked the guard, "May I go now?"

"Yes," the guard replied, "but I'm going to keep my eye on you."

Dad was right, Andy thought. *I* do *get in trouble all the time—even when I don't do anything.* He hurried out of the bathroom and walked quickly to the nearest exhibit hall. He saw lots of paintings and lots of people looking at them, but he didn't see Tamika and Aunt Mandy.

They must wonder where I am, Andy thought, *and I wonder where* they *are.*

"Where are the pressing-nest paintings?" Andy asked a guard.

The guard smiled. "The *Impressionist* paintings are this way," he said, and pointed to the right.

Andy walked past more people and more paintings until he saw Aunt Mandy, Tamika, and Jason standing in front of a large painting of sailboats.

"There you are," Aunt Mandy said. "That was your second time in the bathroom. Are you sick?"

"No," Andy told her. "I feel fine."

"Good," Aunt Mandy said.

Andy turned to Jason and stuck out his tongue. Jason smiled.

Aunt Mandy told the children to walk from

painting to painting, look at each of them, and choose the ones they liked.

Andy and Tamika walked together through the exhibit hall. They stopped in front of a painting of a bowl of fruit.

"What took you so long?" Tamika whispered.

"He wrote *Andy Russell was here!* on the bathroom wall and I had to wash it off."

Tamika said, "He wanted to get you in trouble."

"He *did* get me in trouble! While I was washing it off, a guard walked in."

"Yikes!" Tamika said.

"I'm afraid that guard will tell the woman with the clipboard. She'll think I stuck that sign on Marble Man."

Tamika looked across the exhibit hall at Jason. "He thinks he's funny," Tamika said, "but he's not."

Jason was sitting on a bench in front of a painting of tulips. He had his hands in front of his eyes in open fists, and he was looking through them as if they were binoculars.

"Yesterday," Andy said, "I started a list of clues about who threw out the hamsters. It's a short list. The only clues I have are that they were thrown from a high floor and that whoever did it has fancy handkerchiefs and is good at tying tiny knots. Jason lives on the twentieth floor."

"And he's mean enough to do something like that," Tamika added.

Andy and Tamika watched Jason look through his pretend binoculars.

"And I think whoever tossed the hamsters also put butter on the elevator buttons," Tamika said.

"Aha!" Andy said. "Detective Andy Russell has another clue: When Aunt Mandy pushed the button for the elevator last night, the elevator came down from the twentieth floor. Jason had probably just buttered those buttons." Tamika turned around. Then she turned to one side.

"What are you doing?" Andy asked.

"I'm trying to visualize the apartment to figure out if he lives right above the entrance to the building, because that's where the hamsters came down from." Tamika turned to face Andy. "I think he does."

"So, he's the hamster demon," Andy said. "I'm going to tell Jason we know he did it. If he has any more hamsters—or any pets at all—I'm going to make him give them all to Tom. Someone who tortures hamsters shouldn't be allowed near animals!"

"And he shouldn't butter elevator buttons, either," Tamika said. "But we can't accuse him. He'll just say, 'No, it wasn't me.' We'll have to trick a confession out of him."

Chapter 9
Tamika's Tricks

Andy and Tamika walked slowly toward Jason, but before they reached him, Aunt Mandy said, "Come with me. I want to show you some abstract paintings."

Andy, Tamika, and Jason followed her into a room with just a few huge paintings on each wall. Andy and Tamika sat on a bench in the middle of the room, facing a painting of what looked like overlapping oddly shaped sheets of colored glass.

The plaque below the painting indicated the artist was E. J. Nahum.

"Did you think of a trick?" Andy whispered.

"I will," Tamika replied quietly. "I'll ask him something that has nothing to do with hamsters but will prove he did it. That's what I'll do."

They continued to look at the abstract paintings until Aunt Mandy told them, "It's time for lunch. I know a great place down the street."

Before they left the museum, Jason turned in the numbered tag in return for his backpack. He opened the pack, took a marker from his pocket, and dropped it in.

Andy whispered to Tamika, "That's what he used to write on the bathroom wall."

They left the museum and as they walked to the restaurant, Andy pulled on Jason's backpack.

"Let go," Jason demanded.

Tamika and Aunt Mandy had kept walking. They didn't hear Andy as he whispered to Jason, "You got me in trouble in the museum. I had to wash off what you wrote in the bathroom."

Jason said, "You don't know that I wrote that."

"Yes, I do."

"Well, you can't prove it," Jason countered.

Andy let go of the backpack. Jason hurried to catch up with Aunt Mandy and Tamika. Andy followed close behind.

In the restaurant Aunt Mandy chose a table by the window. A waiter gave each of them a menu.

Andy looked across the table at Jason. Jason smiled and then hid behind his menu.

Aunt Mandy asked for a garden salad and iced tea. Tamika asked for fruit salad and cottage cheese. Jason ordered French toast, with lots of syrup, and orange soda.

"And what would you like?" the waiter asked Andy.

Andy hadn't been thinking about food. He quickly looked at the menu. "I'd like a cheese omelet and milk," he said.

The waiter carried their drinks, a basket of rolls, and a small plate with pats of butter and margarine on it to the table.

While Jason was spreading butter on a roll, Tamika turned to him and asked, "Are the windows in your apartment stuck?"

"That's a strange question," Aunt Mandy said.

"I'm just making polite conversation," Tamika told her aunt. "I was wondering if Jason can open the windows in his apartment. Can you?" she asked him again.

"Why should I?" Jason asked. "We have air-conditioning."

"Hmm," Tamika said.

The waiter brought the salads, omelet, and French toast.

Andy watched Jason pour lots of syrup on his French toast. *Maybe he didn't open his window and throw the hamsters,* Andy thought as he ate a forkful of omelet. *Maybe he has a balcony, like Aunt Mandy, and threw them from there.*

When they were done eating, Aunt Mandy looked at her watch. "We should get going," she said. "We don't want to be late for the ballet."

"May I take a few rolls for later?" Jason asked the waiter. "I might get hungry."

The waiter said he could.

"Take butter, too," Tamika told him. "You could put it on the roll—or on some elevator buttons."

Aunt Mandy turned and glared at Tamika.

"Butter will make a mess in my backpack," Jason said as he put a few rolls in it.

They took a taxicab to the ballet, and on the way, Jason slumped low in the backseat. He looked to the side, away from Andy, Tamika, and Aunt Mandy. When the taxicab stopped, Andy gazed up at the tall marble columns at the front of the theater. Beyond the columns were large windows. Andy looked through the windows and saw a huge crystal chandelier.

Aunt Mandy and the children got out of the cab. Tamika, Andy, and Jason followed Aunt Mandy into the theater.

Andy looked up at the chandelier. It seemed to him like he was standing beneath thousands of large glass snowflakes. "This is some nice place," he said to Aunt Mandy. "Just look at that chandelier!"

Aunt Mandy, Tamika, and Jason looked up.

"Those sure are lots of pieces of glass," Tamika said to Jason. "And do you know how they keep all those pieces of glass up there?"

Jason didn't answer.

"I'll bet they're all tied together with thin pieces

of thread or wire in tiny knots," Tamika said. Then she asked Jason, "Can *you* tie tiny knots?"

Tiny knots, Andy thought, and remembered the hamsters and the handkerchiefs tied to their feet. Whenever he thought about those small animals being mistreated that way, Andy got upset.

Jason smiled.

"Why should I tie tiny knots?" he asked. "I'm not making a chandelier."

"You're asking some very strange questions," Aunt Mandy said.

"She sure is," Jason agreed.

"She sure is!" Tamika mimicked Jason, then she whispered to Andy as they followed Aunt Mandy and Jason up the stairs. "I ask strange questions because he does strange things. And did you see him smile when I asked about the tiny knots? That proves he's the one."

Andy told Tamika, "It doesn't prove anything except that you didn't trick Jason."

Aunt Mandy and the children followed an usher to their seats in the very first row of the mezzanine, overlooking the stage. Jason stood against the rail and watched the people below in the orchestra level going to their seats. He took a roll from his backpack and held it out over the rail.

Andy stood next to him and looked down, too.

Jason squeezed the roll. Crumbs fell onto the head of a woman in a red dress. She brushed the crumbs off and looked around. Then she looked up and saw Andy. She angrily waved her pointing finger at him.

Andy looked for Jason. He was sitting next to Aunt Mandy.

I'm in trouble again for something Jason did! Andy thought.

Tamika was sitting on the other side of Aunt Mandy. Andy walked over and sat down next to Tamika.

"Have you ever seen a ballet?" Aunt Mandy asked.

Tamika shook her head. She had never seen a ballet.

"I saw one," Andy said. "I saw *Swan Lake.*"

"Did you like it?" Aunt Mandy asked.

"Well . . . ," Andy said slowly. He didn't think Aunt Mandy wanted to hear that he'd watched it on television—and that he'd tuned in because he

liked animals and he'd thought *Swan Lake* would be about swans. "It wasn't what I expected," Andy said.

"We're seeing *Sleeping Beauty*," Aunt Mandy said. "Do you know the story of *Sleeping Beauty*?"

"Is that the fairy tale about the Goldie girl and the bears?" Jason asked.

"It's about a beautiful princess," Tamika told him. "She's cursed by a wicked fairy—that she will stick her finger with a needle and die."

"That's right," Aunt Mandy said.

Tamika asked Jason, "Do you like fairy tales?" Jason hesitated.

Andy watched Jason and thought, *He's trying to figure out what's the trick in that question—so am I.*

"Yes . . . ," Jason answered slowly. "I like some fairy tales."

"Do you like *animal* tails—small furry animal tails?" Tamika asked.

The theater lights dimmed.

"You can talk later," Aunt Mandy said, with a puzzled look on her face. "There will be two short intermissions."

Chapter 10
Look What Someone Did

The orchestra played soft music. The curtains opened. Andy sat back and watched the prologue and first act of *Sleeping Beauty*.

Listening to the music was relaxing. Andy's eyes slowly closed.

Suddenly there was a thunderlike noise and flashing lights.

Andy quickly opened his eyes. *Oops!* he thought. *I've got to keep my eyes open. Aunt Mandy might ask questions.*

Andy sat forward in his seat and tried to follow the story.

I wish one of those dancers would talk so I'd know what's happening, Andy thought.

At the end of the first act, the princess pretended to prick her finger. She fell to the floor of the stage. The king's men carried Princess Aurora to the castle and everyone fell asleep.

The theater lights went on.

Andy looked at the people below in the orchestra level. Many were standing by their seats. Some were in the aisles, walking toward the exits.

Jason grabbed his backpack. Then he told Aunt Mandy, "I have to go to the bathroom."

Tamika tugged on Andy's shirt. "You'd better go with him," she said.

"Oh, I have to go, too," Andy told Aunt Mandy.

Jason pushed through the people in the aisle. He seemed to be in a real hurry, and he bumped into lots of people on his way to the exit.

"Please, excuse me," Andy said as he tried to avoid bumping into people. "Please, excuse me," he repeated as he hurried through the exit archway.

Men and women were standing and talking in

groups in the mezzanine lobby. Others were walking down the wide staircase, to the orchestra level of the theater. Some people were standing on the other side of the lobby, by a small counter, buying beverages. Andy looked at all the people, but he didn't find Jason. He went into the bathroom. Jason wasn't there.

When he returned to the mezzanine lobby, Andy saw Tamika. "I can't find him," he said. "He's disappeared."

"Maybe he's back in his seat," Tamika suggested.

As Andy and Tamika walked toward the front of the mezzanine, Andy felt something soft land on his head. He brushed it off.

"Bread!" he said as a piece fell to the floor.

There were lots of bread crumbs on the floor.

Andy and Tamika looked up. The edge of the balcony was right above them.

Andy told Tamika, "That has to be Jason."

The lights flickered.

"We must get back to our seats," Tamika said. "The ballet is going to start again."

"Jason likes to throw things from balconies of theaters," Andy said. "Maybe he likes to throw things from windows or balconies of apartment buildings, too. I'm adding this to my list of clues."

Andy and Tamika returned to their seats. Then as the lights dimmed, Jason sat down next to Aunt Mandy.

"You're just in time," she whispered to Jason.

Andy tried to watch the dancers on the stage during the second act, but he kept thinking about Jason. *What would one of those TV detectives do?* Andy wondered. But before he could answer his own question, the theater lights went on again.

People throughout the theater stood and turned to go to the lobby during the second intermission.

Andy turned, too. "Oh my," he said to Tamika. "Look!" Andy pointed. "Look at what someone did."

Chapter 11
So What?

Something green and stringy was hanging from the edge of the balcony.

"What is that?" Andy asked.

"Let's take a look," Tamika said.

As Andy and Tamika started toward the back of the theater, Jason said, "I'm thirsty. I need a drink."

"Let's all get drinks," Aunt Mandy said cheerfully.

Jason grabbed his backpack and followed Aunt

Mandy, Tamika, and Andy up the aisle. It was a wide aisle, but people were walking single file. No one wanted to walk into the green stringy stuff hanging from the balcony.

Jason was smiling.

"That's terrible," Aunt Mandy said. "Who would do such a thing?"

"And how did *he* do it?" Tamika asked.

Jason took a few steps back and looked up. "He or *she* probably went upstairs, leaned over the rail, and sprayed from a can of stringy foam," he said.

Andy said, "And I know where he keeps that can of stringy foam—he keeps it in his backpack." He reached for Jason's pack.

"What are you doing?" Aunt Mandy asked Andy. "That belongs to Jason."

"He can look in here," Jason replied, handing Andy his backpack.

Andy reached into the backpack. There was no can. "Here," Andy said, returning the pack to Jason.

Aunt Mandy and the three children went to the refreshment counter in the mezzanine lobby.

"I want orange soda," Jason said to the man behind the counter.

Andy and Tamika told Aunt Mandy they weren't thirsty.

Aunt Mandy and Jason walked away from the counter, to a corner of the lobby.

Tamika held on to Andy's sleeve, signaling him to stay behind. "Well, Detective Russell, my tricks didn't work," she said. "Now what do we do?"

" 'What do we do?' " Andy repeated. He pointed to his own head and said, "I guess I *am* a good detective after all. What we just proved is that Jason *did* spray the foam."

"We did?" Tamika asked.

"Yes," Andy said. "This morning the guard looked inside the backpack and told Jason he couldn't take it into the museum. That's because there *was* something suspicious in there, but it's not there anymore because Jason used it up."

"You mean something like a can of stringy foam?" Tamika asked.

"Exactly!" Andy said. "Jason must have leaned over the rail of the balcony and sprayed it. When the can was empty, he threw it out. He thought that by showing us the empty backpack, he'd tricked us—but he really tricked himself."

"That's right," Tamika said. "And the rolls

weren't in there because he broke them into crumbs and dropped them on people."

Andy and Tamika looked at Jason. He was drinking his soda.

Andy said, "I'm going to have to do what the TV detectives do. I'll *make* him confess."

The lights flickered again.

Andy and Tamika followed Jason and Aunt Mandy to their seats.

While everyone else watched the third act of *Sleeping Beauty,* Andy watched Jason. He wondered how he could make him admit that he'd thrown the hamsters out the window.

When the ballet ended, almost everybody in the theater stood and applauded as the dancers took their bows. After the curtain closed, Aunt Mandy and the children followed the crowd up the aisle and out of the mezzanine.

Tamika thanked her aunt for taking them to the ballet. Andy and Jason thanked her, too.

"I really enjoyed spending the day with such good children," Aunt Mandy said.

Good? Andy thought. *Jason is not good at all. Sometimes I wonder if adults have any idea what's really going on in this world.*

In the orchestra-level lobby a woman in a red dress turned and saw Andy.

Oh no, Andy thought. *I'm in trouble again.*

The woman pointed at Andy. "That's *him!*" she said loudly to the man next to her. "That's the boy who leaned over the mezzanine rail and dropped bread crumbs onto my hair."

"Excuse me, but it couldn't have been him," Aunt Mandy told the woman. "He didn't bring any bread into the theater." Then Aunt Mandy looked at Jason and said, "But this boy did."

Jason smiled at the woman.

"That's true," he told her. "I *did* bring some rolls into the theater. If some crumbs dropped on your head while I was eating, I'm sorry."

"Hmm." The woman grunted and walked off.

"When you leaned over the rail, you weren't eating a roll," Aunt Mandy said. "You deliberately dropped crumbs on that woman, didn't you?"

Jason didn't answer.

"And you wrote my name on the wall of the museum bathroom," Andy said, accusing Jason. "I got in trouble for that—I had to wash the marker off."

"You did?" Aunt Mandy asked. When Jason didn't answer, she knew that he had.

"And the worst thing you did," Andy said, "was throw hamsters out of your window!"

"You did that, too?" Aunt Mandy asked. "That's horrible!"

Andy and Aunt Mandy were talking really loudly. People in the crowded lobby turned to look.

"I didn't *throw* the hamsters out the window," Jason said. "I dropped them off the balcony, and I knew they wouldn't be hurt because before I dropped them, I tested my handkerchief parachutes with tomatoes and toothpicks. The tomatoes weren't hurt, so I knew the hamsters would be OK, too."

"They were so scared," Andy said.

"Not that you even care, Jason, but Tom has the hamsters now," Tamika said. "They're all crowded in a wooden box."

Aunt Mandy grabbed Jason's hand. She pulled him toward the exit. "I'm getting you home," she said. "I don't want to be responsible for you anymore. I don't even want to be with someone who

annoys people with bread crumbs, defaces a museum, and tortures animals."

The children were quiet during the taxicab ride home. In the elevator of the apartment building, before she pressed the button to go up, Aunt Mandy asked Jason, "Are you the one who put butter on the elevator buttons?"

"It wasn't butter," Jason answered quietly. "It was *margarine*."

"And you thought that was funny?" Aunt Mandy asked.

Jason didn't answer.

Aunt Mandy pressed the elevator button for the twentieth floor. When the doors opened, everyone got off.

While they were standing at the door to Jason's apartment, Aunt Mandy looked at Jason. "First, you owe all of us an apology," she said firmly.

"I'm sorry," Jason told Aunt Mandy. Then he apologized to Andy and Tamika.

Aunt Mandy told Jason, "And those hamsters don't have to live crowded in a box. Do you have a cage and food for them?"

"Sure I do. Do you want to buy them?" replied Jason.

"That's not your cage and it's not your food," Andy said angrily. "They belong to the hamsters." Jason looked at Aunt Mandy.

"That's right," Aunt Mandy said. "They belong to the hamsters. Just go get them."

Jason knocked on the door to his apartment. His mother opened the door.

Jason hurried to his room.

Jason's mother thanked Aunt Mandy for taking him to the museum and the ballet.

Aunt Mandy looked at Jason's mother. Aunt Mandy seemed like she was about to say something—but she didn't.

Jason returned with a hamster cage, a bag of food, and hamster toys. He gave all the things to Andy and Tamika.

"These are for Tom," Jason explained to his mother. "He has the hamsters now, and he needs this stuff."

"Oh, you gave the hamsters to Tom," Jason's mother said. "That's so nice of you."

Before Andy or Tamika could respond, Jason's mother turned to Aunt Mandy. "I hope that the next time you take your niece and her friend somewhere, you'll take Jason along, too," she said.

Aunt Mandy said, "I don't think so."

Jason's mother was surprised by Aunt Mandy's answer. She waited for an explanation.

"Speak to Jason," Aunt Mandy said. "He can tell you why."

Andy, Tamika, and Aunt Mandy waited.

"I got into some mischief at the museum and at the ballet," Jason said quietly.

"I'm so sorry," Jason's mother told Aunt Mandy. Then she turned to Jason. "We need to talk."

"Ask him about the hamsters, margarine, and bread crumbs," Aunt Mandy said.

"All that?" Jason's mother asked.

"Yes," Aunt Mandy answered as she led Andy and Tamika toward the elevator. "And the bathroom walls, too."

Andy, Tamika, and Aunt Mandy went to Tom's office in the underground garage. The WHITE ZINFANDEL box was on Tom's desk.

"Look—babies!" Tom said.

Six tiny hamsters were cuddled with their mother.

"I love watching them," Tom said. He saw all the things Andy and Tamika had brought for the hamsters. "Let's leave the mother and her babies in the box. But we can move the others."

Aunt Mandy and the children helped.

Andy watched as Aunt Mandy lifted a hamster and put it in the cage. He was impressed by how gentle she was.

"I plan to keep the hamsters here," Tom told the children. "You can visit them anytime you want.

"And if you come to our house, you can visit my gerbils; my snake, Slither; and my goldfish, Sylvia," Andy told Aunt Mandy and Tom.

Chapter 12
Trouble?

When Aunt Mandy opened the door to her apartment, Andy took another look at the two large paintings in the entrance area. He looked at them for a while.

When he had first seen the large blotches of blue surrounded by other colors, Andy had thought the paintings were upside down—or inside out. Now, when he looked at the paintings again, he liked them.

"Aren't they beautiful?" Aunt Mandy asked. "The artist is E. J. Nahum."

"Isn't that the guy who did some of the paintings we saw in the museum?" Andy asked.

"Yes," Aunt Mandy answered proudly. "Now wash up, and then we'll eat."

Andy didn't think he was dirty, but he washed his hands anyway. Then he followed Tamika into the dining room.

The lights were dim. Aunt Mandy was sitting at the table, which was beautifully set with a white cloth; gold-trimmed dishes; silver knives, spoons, and forks; tall glasses—and with two lit candles in candlesticks at the center of the table.

Uncle Terence walked in. He was wearing a tuxedo, and his hair was plastered down. He told Aunt Mandy, Andy, and Tamika to sit down, and he gave them each a menu. Then he folded his hands, looked up at the ceiling, and said, "Good evening. My name is Terence. I will be your waiter."

Andy, Tamika, and Aunt Mandy looked at Uncle Terence and laughed.

Andy thought that Uncle Terence, with his plastered-down hair, looked a little like Jacques.

But Jacques looks like a short, fat penguin, and Uncle Terence looks like a tall, thin one!

Uncle Terence stared at the ceiling and waited.

Aunt Mandy leaned over the table and whispered to Andy and Tamika, "I think we should look at our menus and decide what we want."

Andy held his menu up, by the candlelight, so he could read it.

There were only four items on the menu:

PANCAKES WITH SYRUP

PANCAKES WITH APPLESAUCE

PANCAKES WITH STRAWBERRIES

PANCAKES WITH PANCAKES

"You know what?" Aunt Mandy laughed and said, "I think I'll have breakfast food for dinner. I'll have pancakes!"

"Me, too," Andy and Tamika agreed.

Uncle Terence brought in a large platter of pancakes, bottles of syrup, jars of applesauce, and a bowl of strawberries. He unbuttoned his jacket; took off his bow tie; sat down with Andy, Tamika, and Aunt Mandy; and ate dinner.

The next morning Mr. Russell came to pick up Andy and Tamika.

Aunt Mandy invited him to sit on the balcony. She brought out a plate of the icing-covered cubes with candy sprinkles.

Andy whispered to his father, "You should eat those—there's cake inside and they're really good. Everything here is really good!"

When it was time to leave, Andy and Tamika thanked Aunt Mandy and Uncle Terence.

"I had a great time," Andy said.

"I did, too," Tamika told them.

"We hope you'll come again," Aunt Mandy and Uncle Terence said.

As they drove away from the apartment building, Andy looked at all the tall buildings; the cars, taxis, and buses; and the sidewalks crowded with people. *I really had a good time this weekend,* he thought.

When Mr. Russell stopped at a traffic light, he turned and asked Andy, "Did you get into any trouble at Aunt Mandy's?"

"Trouble?" Andy replied slowly. "Well, I got into lots of trouble—but I got out of it."

"None of it was his fault," Tamika said. "You can even call Aunt Mandy. She really liked Andy and so did Uncle Terence. They said they hope he'll visit again."

"Yes, they did say that," Mr. Russell said as the light turned green and he drove off. "Now, please, tell me about the trouble."

Andy and Tamika took turns telling Mr. Russell everything that had happened at Aunt Mandy's.

When they were done, Mr. Russell shook his head and said to Andy, "I just don't know why you always get into such trouble."

Andy was looking out the car window. He turned to his father and said, "I don't, either, Dad. I really don't."